Dear Parents:

Congratulations! Your child is taking the first steps on an exciting journey. The destination? Independent reading!

STEP INTO READING® will help your child get there. The program offers five steps to reading success. Each step includes fun stories and colorful art or photographs. In addition to original fiction and books with favorite characters, there are Step into Reading Non-Fiction Readers, Phonics Readers and Boxed Sets, Sticker Readers, and Comic Readers—a complete literacy program with something to interest every child.

Learning to Read, Step by Step!

Ready to Read   Preschool–Kindergarten
• big type and easy words • rhyme and rhythm • picture clues
For children who know the alphabet and are eager to begin reading.

Reading with Help   Preschool–Grade 1
• basic vocabulary • short sentences • simple stories
For children who recognize familiar words and sound out new words with help.

Reading on Your Own   Grades 1–3
• engaging characters • easy-to-follow plots • popular topics
For children who are ready to read on their own.

Reading Paragraphs   Grades 2–3
• challenging vocabulary • short paragraphs • exciting stories
For newly independent readers who read simple sentences with confidence.

Ready for Chapters   Grades 2–4
• chapters • longer paragraphs • full-color art
For children who want to take the plunge into chapter books but still like colorful pictures.

STEP INTO READING® is designed to give every child a successful reading experience. The grade levels are only guides; children will progress through the steps at their own speed, developing confidence in their reading.

Remember, a lifetime love of reading starts with a single step!

Visit us on the Web!
StepIntoReading.com
rhcbooks.com

Educators and librarians, for a variety of teaching tools, visit us at RHTeachersLibrarians.com

ISBN 978-1-5247-7273-4 (trade) — ISBN 978-1-5247-7274-1 (lib. bdg.)

Printed in the United States of America

10 9 8 7 6 5 4 3 2 1

THE GREAT MONKEY SHOW!

RUSTY RIVETS

adapted by Delphine Finnegan

based on the teleplay
"Monkey Mayhem" by Ron Holsey

illustrated by Donald Cassity

Random House 🏠 New York

Rusty and Ruby
visit the Animal Park.
They want to see
the monkey show!

Ranger Anna

has a problem.

The monkeys are bored.

They will not perform.

Ruby has an idea.

She and Rusty

will create a new act!

Ranger Anna leaves
to feed the seals.
Rusty and Ruby stay
with the monkeys.

Rusty and Ruby
try to think
of a new act
for the monkeys.

But they have a problem.

The monkeys escape!

Rusty and Ruby follow
them into town.
They find the monkeys
juggling apples.

The monkeys run away!
They take Rusty's go-kart
and Ruby's buggy.

They take Officer Carl's hovercycle, too!

Rusty and Ruby
chase the monkeys.
They find them
in the park.

The monkeys
spin and flip.

They climb up high.

At the ice cream shop,
the monkeys bang drums
and dance to the beat.

Rusty and Ruby
have a great idea
for the monkeys' new act!

Rusty, Ruby, and
the Bits get to work.
The monkeys help.

They make the
Drum-o-matic Monkey-tastic
Showstopper 5000!
Soon it is time for
the show.

The monkeys juggle.

They bang on the drums.

They love the
new invention!

The crowd claps and
cheers for the monkeys.

Everyone loves

their new act!

The great monkey show
is a hit, thanks to Rusty,
Ruby, and the Bits!